For my family and friends and, of course, the dog

First published in the United States by
Ideals Publishing Corporation
Nelson Place at Elm Hill Pike
Nashville, Tennessee 37214

Copyright © 1989 by Cliff Wright

First published in Great Britain in 1989 by Hutchinson Children's
Books, Covent Garden, London

Printed and bound in Italy

ISBN 0-8249-8443-9

WHEN THE WORLD SLEEPS

Cliff Wright

IDEALS CHILDREN'S BOOKS
Nashville, Tennessee

One night, when the world
was asleep, something
magical happened. No one
knew of it, except one small
boy who chanced to wake . . .

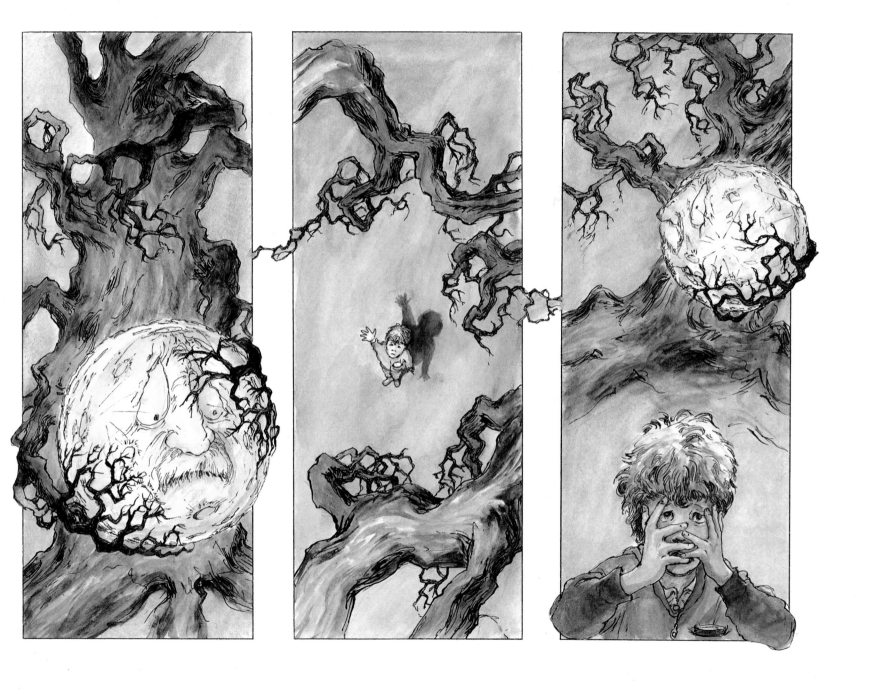